The

LIGHTHOUSE FAMILY

THE SEA LION

The
LIGHTHOUSE FAMILY

THE SEA LION

BY CYNTHIA RYLANT

ILLUSTRATED BY PRESTON McDANIELS

J
Fic
Rylant
2017

BEACH LANE BOOKS
New York London Toronto Sydney New Delhi

BEACH LANE BOOKS
An imprint of Simon & Schuster Children's Publishing Division
1230 Avenue of the Americas, New York, New York 10020
This book is a work of fiction. Any references to historical events, real people,
or real places are used fictitiously. Other names, characters, places, and events
are products of the author's imagination, and any resemblance to actual events
or places or persons, living or dead, is entirely coincidental.
Text copyright © 2017 by Cynthia Rylant
Illustrations copyright © 2017 by Preston McDaniels
All rights reserved, including the right of reproduction in whole or in part in any form.
BEACH LANE BOOKS is a trademark of Simon & Schuster, Inc.
For information about special discounts for bulk purchases, please contact Simon &
Schuster Special Sales at 1-866-506-1949 or business@simonandschuster.com.
The Simon & Schuster Speakers Bureau can bring authors to your live event.
For more information or to book an event, contact the Simon & Schuster Speakers
Bureau at 1-866-248-3049 or visit our website at www.simonspeakers.com.
The text for this book was set in Centaur.
The illustrations for this book were rendered in graphite.
Manufactured in the United States of America
0217 PCH
First Edition
2 4 6 8 10 9 7 5 3 1
CIP data for this book is available from the Library of Congress.
ISBN 9781481460255
ISBN 9781481460279 (eBook)

For Peanut
—P. McD.

CONTENTS

1. *Fall Days*

There stands above the dark blue sea a solitary lighthouse that once was the home of only a solitary lightkeeper, Pandora the cat. Pandora had pledged her life to the protection of all the sailing ships. Faithfully, night and day, she tended the lights, and she did her best not to feel lonely. But this was not always easy.

Then one day Pandora's life changed completely when a storm threw onto her shore a sailor named Seabold and his broken little boat, *Adventure*. Pandora had company!

She helped Seabold regain his health, and she watched as he repaired his boat to return to the sea. A good-bye was near at hand.

But before Seabold could set sail, there was yet another rescue. Pandora and Seabold found three orphaned children drifting in a crate in the sea, afraid and hungry. Their names were Whistler, Lila, and Tiny, and they very much needed a home.

They found one. Not only a home with Pandora in the protection of her lighthouse. But, remarkably, a home with Seabold as well. For the noble sailor came to care about them so much that he decided to stay, to help look after them, and to be of use.

And this is how the lighthouse family was made.

Fall was a beautiful time of year at the lighthouse. Out at sea the gray whales migrating south blew heart-shaped spray to say hello to Pandora, for they had known the kind cat for many years. Blueberries growing in

deep thickets attracted thousands of swallows who swooped down for a big meal before flying to catch up with the whales. And in the evenings, sunsets cast a deep red glow over all the windows of the tall tower.

Summers were always playful times for the lighthouse family, but in the fall Pandora and Seabold got serious about lightkeeping again. Any day now there would be the first fog of the season, and the windows and the prisms in the lantern room had to be spotless. Seabold was always going up and down the ladder with polishing rags in his hands. Pandora passed pails of lantern oil to him for the

giant lamp that burned each evening to warn sailors away from the dangerous rocks.

Because the children had only a short time left for playing safely outside before winter arrived, Pandora urged them to go and explore.

"Are you sure you don't need us to polish?" Whistler asked as he and Lila headed for the door every day.

"No, my dears," said Pandora. "Your work is to play."

Whistler and Lila smiled. It was nice to have that sort of work.

The children then left the cottage and their baby sister, Tiny, who enjoyed being the baby in the house, and they went out to see what they might find. Pandora sent them with pockets full of special candies made of cherries and lavender flowers.

"To keep you nicely fed until supper," she said.

Whistler and Lila loved to explore. There were so many different places to go, and one never knew what one might find.

This day Whistler and Lila saw a snowy owl perching at the very top of a high sand dune, surveying all the land and sea.

"He is thinking about the great wide world," said Whistler. Lila nodded. They were both admirers of the owl, whom they saw now and then. Soon the owl would fly back to the Arctic, Seabold had told them. But at present he was here.

The children climbed the rocky slopes covered with wild roses, heading for the secret cove used by the whale mothers as a day-nursery for their babies. The babies swam in circles while the mothers went away for a little while to do whatever mother whales do.

Whistler and Lila hoped somebody might be in the cove today, but there were no baby whales, only some black-tailed deer enjoying a bite of kelp on the rocks.

The polite children tried to be very quiet so as not to disturb the deer, but they walked over a patch of rockweed, and it made a loud *pop-pop-pop* when they did.

The deer saw them and ran away. Deer were always shy.

"So sorry!" called Lila.

"Sorry!" said Whistler.

But there were others who did enjoy the children's company. On the mudflats the sea scallops loved being chased by the children. When Whistler and Lila reached down to tag a scallop, it forced a jet of water from its shell that doused the children and set it spinning.

Whistler and Lila got very wet from so many showers, and they laughed all the way home.

"You've been visiting the scallops again,"

Pandora said, smiling as she helped them remove their wet sweaters. The children changed into dry clothes, then sat at the table eating big bowls of beet and barley stew. Baby Tiny was asleep in a tea tin filled with moss.

It was another very nice day at the lighthouse. But the children still hoped someone new might come along soon to give them an adventure.

And someone did.

2. A Baby!

In the cottage, Pandora was always the first one up in the mornings, as she enjoyed having a quiet kitchen to herself while she prepared the family's breakfast. Stirring up a big pot of porridge at dawn made her happy.

So it was Pandora who exclaimed "My goodness!" rather loudly on the morning that someone new arrived. And this woke everyone up except the visitor himself.

In their nightgowns and slippers, the lighthouse family stared at the visitor asleep in Seabold's chair.

It was a baby sea lion, snoring in perfect contentment.

"Should we wake him?" asked Lila, very much looking forward to a new playmate.

All eyes turned to Seabold. Since it was his chair, everyone seemed to think this was his decision.

Seabold shook his head.

"Let the baby sleep," Seabold told them. "Goodness knows I've sawed plenty of logs in that chair myself."

"Sawed logs?" repeated Whistler.

Seabold smiled. "Snored," he said.

So the family went about having their breakfast, and in spite of pans rattling and this and that dropping to the floor and many requests to pass the maple syrup, the baby sea lion, as all babies do, slept soundly through the noise of a very busy home.

Then finally, as Whistler and Lila were drying the last two breakfast plates, the sea lion opened his eyes.

He saw Tiny playing with a set of wooden blocks on the kitchen table, and he sat up in Seabold's chair, clapped both flippers, and roared like a lion.

"Heavens!" said everyone. Tiny laughed at the other baby, who could roar.

Once everyone's nerves had settled (they were not used to someone roaring in their kitchen), and welcomes had all been said, the family learned that the sea lion's name was Topper and that his mother had brought him to the cottage, put him in Seabold's chair, and told him to "wait here."

"For how long?" asked Whistler.

Suddenly the baby sea lion's eyes filled with tears.

"Oh, not long at all, I'm sure!" said Lila quickly to reassure the baby. "Not long at all!"

"Would you like a bowl of porridge?" she asked. Lila had always been good with babies. Her own baby sister adored her.

Topper wiped his eyes and nodded his head.

Sitting there in Seabold's chair, silver whiskers just like Seabold's, he seemed almost like another member of the family. A little Seabold.

And Topper did fit in beautifully. He ate what the children ate, played when the children played (he was quite good at catch), and napped when the children napped. Staying busy helped keep away Topper's worries about how long he might have to wait for his mother.

The family enjoyed Topper very much. And Topper was curious about everything, so he would hold something in his flippers and ask, "What's this?" Then he would throw whatever it was into the air and bark at it. Tiny loved this. She clapped and clapped, which made Topper do it even more.

Topper had been at the lighthouse for three days before Pandora and Seabold found out that the baby sea lion had not yet learned how to swim.

"Oh dear," said Pandora.

"My mother was just about to teach me," said Topper, "before she told me to wait here."

Pandora had a very strong motherly instinct, so she wanted Topper to learn to swim as soon as possible.

"It is important for a sea lion," she told him.

There was an old dugout canoe behind the lighthouse that had been sitting in the tall grass for many years. The canoe was never used, for Seabold had his own boat, and the only river for paddling was too far away. So it was not very useful as a canoe.

But it would be a perfect baby pool.

So while they waited for Topper's mother to return, the lighthouse family saw to it that Topper had some swimming lessons.

3. *Mary's Return*

On the seventh day of the baby sea lion's stay, news finally arrived. It arrived in the form of a flock of very loud geese flying in a V above Seabold's head as he repaired a gate latch in the garden.

The geese were all shouting the news so loudly that it was impossible for Seabold to hear anyone because he had to listen to everyone.

When this became apparent to the geese, a representative landed.

"Topper's mother had to give an injured puffin a ride to Hadley's Atoll," said the goose. "But she's on her way back. She'll be here tomorrow."

This was indeed wonderful news. So wonderful that Whistler and Lila decided to decorate the cottage porch for the mother's arrival. They gathered angelwing shells from the clay of the salt marsh and strung them from post to post. Then they used Whistler's collection of old sand dollars to spell out WELCOME above the front door.

Best of all, Lila sewed a navy-blue sailor cap for Topper to wear for his mother's return.

The following day Topper's mother arrived just as she had promised. She was a very large sea lion, and her silver whiskers were much longer than Topper's. Lila thought she was beautiful.

Her name was Mary. From the sea Mary had watched the lighthouse family for a long time. And when she needed suddenly to help her puffin friend home, she knew that her baby would be safe at the lighthouse. Which, of course, he was.

"I am so grateful," said Mary. "I hope Topper didn't bark too much."

"Oh no," said Seabold. "And besides, barking is music to the ears."

To thank them all, Mary had brought a pretty basket woven of bear grass. (The puffin's brother was a basket weaver.) Pandora filled the basket with figs and plums and honey buns.

Then everyone followed a very happy little sea lion to the back of the cottage.

And they all watched him swim.

CYNTHIA RYLANT lives in Oregon, not far from the Pacific Ocean, and PRESTON MCDANIELS lives on the Great Plains in Aurora, Nebraska.